This Walker book belongs to:

_____

_____

_____

First published 1986 by Walker Books Ltd
87 Vauxhall Walk, London SE11 5HJ

This edition published 2010 for Index Books Ltd

2 4 6 8 10 9 7 5 3 1

© 1986 Colin West

The right of Colin West to be identified as author/illustrator of this work has been asserted by him
in accordance with the Copyright, Designs and Patents Act 1988

This book has been typeset in Optima

Printed in China

British Library Cataloguing in Publication Data:
a catalogue record for this book is available from the British Library

ISBN 978-1-4063-2104-3

www.walker.co.uk

# "Pardon?" said the giraffe

## Colin West

WALKER BOOKS

AND SUBSIDIARIES

LONDON • BOSTON • SYDNEY • AUCKLAND

"What's it like up there?"
  asked the frog
    as he hopped on the ground.

"Pardon?" said the giraffe.

"What's it like up there?"
asked the frog
as he hopped on the lion.

"Pardon?"
said the
giraffe.

"What's it like up there?"
   asked the frog
   as he hopped on the hippo.

"Pardon?"
said the
giraffe.

"What's it like up there?"
    asked the frog
    as he hopped on the elephant.

"Pardon?"
said the
giraffe.

"What's it like up there?"
    asked the frog
    as he hopped on the giraffe.

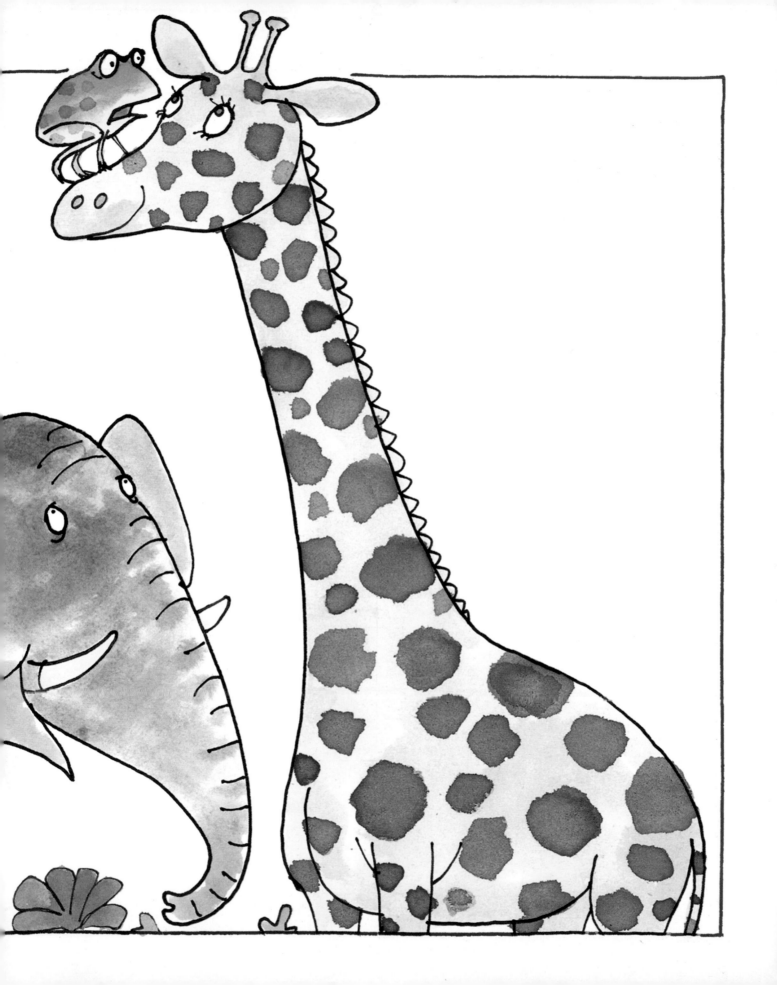

"It's nice up here, thank you,"
   said the giraffe,
"but you're tickling my nose
   and I think I'm going to..."

A-A-A-TISHOOOO

Colin West says that the idea for *"Pardon?" said the Giraffe*
came to him because he wanted to write a story
about animals of different heights.
He says, "A giraffe is the natural choice for a tall animal,
while a frog provided me with a good, cheeky, small character.
'What's it like up there?' is a phrase rather tall people often
have to put up with. In my story I think the giraffe can
hear the question perfectly well, but she is determined to
wear out the rude frog as he hops higher and higher."